OLIVIA™
and Her Ducklings

adapted by Veera Hiranandani
based on the screenplay written by Eryk Casemiro and Kate Boutiler
illustrated by Shane L. Johnson

Ready-to-Read

Simon Spotlight
New York   London   Toronto   Sydney

Based on the TV series *OLIVIA*™ as seen on Nickelodeon™

SIMON SPOTLIGHT
An imprint of Simon & Schuster Children's Publishing Division
1230 Avenue of the Americas, New York, New York 10020
First Simon Spotlight hardcover edition August 2010
Copyright © 2009 Silver Lining Productions Limited (a Chorion company). All rights reserved. OLIVIA™ and
© 2009 Ian Falconer. All rights reserved
All rights reserved, including the right of reproduction in whole or in part in any form
SIMON SPOTLIGHT, READY-TO-READ, and colophon are registered trademarks of Simon & Schuster, Inc
For information about special discounts for bulk purchases, please contact Simon & Schuster Special
Sales at 1-866-506-1949 or business@simonandschuster.com
Manufactured in the United States of America 0710 LAK
1 2 3 4 5 6 7 8 9 10
The Library of Congress has cataloged the paperback edition as follows
Hiranandani, Veera
Olivia and her ducklings / adapted by Veera Hiranandani ; based on a teleplay by Eryk Casemiro and Kate
Boutilier. — 1st ed
p. cm. — (Ready-to-read
"Based on the TV series, Olivia as seen on Nickelodeon"—C.p
I. Casemiro, Eryk. II. Boutilier, Kate. III. Olivia (Television program) IV. Title
PZ7.H5977325OI 2010   [E]—dc22   2009007381
ISBN 978-1-4169-9079-6 (pbk
ISBN 978-1-4424-1382-5 (hc

is painting a picture of .

OLIVIA   IAN

But will not stand still.

IAN

He has an itchy nose.

OLIVIA looks for something else

to paint.

She sees some **DUCKS** .

Maybe she can paint

a picture of them.

"Poor little  ,"

says OLIVIA .

"They want their mother."

The  cannot climb the

The **DUCKS** cannot climb the **HILL** and **OLIVIA** and **IAN** help them.

"Come on,  !" says  .

DUCKS OLIVIA

"Quack!" says  .

IAN

They did it!
 OLIVIA wants to stay with
the  DUCKS .
But it is time to go home.
"Good-bye, DUCKS ! " says OLIVIA .

At home,  paints

OLIVIA

a picture of [FLOWERS] .

FLOWERS

She paints her [FLOWERS]

FLOWERS

[RED] , [YELLOW] , and [PINK] .

RED   YELLOW   PINK

Quack!

"Very funny,  IAN. Please stop," says  OLIVIA.

"Stop what?" asks  IAN.

"Look!" says .
OLIVIA

"The followed us home!"
DUCKS

"I guess they really, really like me!"  says.

"Quack!" say the  .

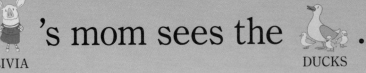's mom sees the .

OLIVIA   DUCKS

"Can we keep them?"

asks .

OLIVIA

"I'm sorry, 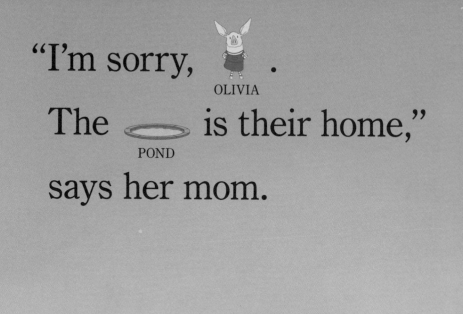.
The is their home,"
says her mom.

looks in the living room.

But she does not see any .

 OLIVIA cannot find
the  DUCKS .
"  IAN ! Please help
me!" calls  OLIVIA .

"! I know where
OLIVIA
the ![ducks] are!
DUCKS
Come to the bathroom!"
says ![ian].
IAN

The  DUCKS are in the bathtub! "Just because I hate baths doesn't mean DUCKS hate them too," says IAN.

After their swim,
it is time for bed.
"Would you like me to read
you a  ?"

BOOK

asks the .

OLIVIA

DUCKS

But the  are asleep.
DUCKS
"Good night, ducks ," says OLIVIA .
Soon OLIVIA will be asleep too.

"The  have to

go back in the morning,"

her mom says.

DUCKS

At least the 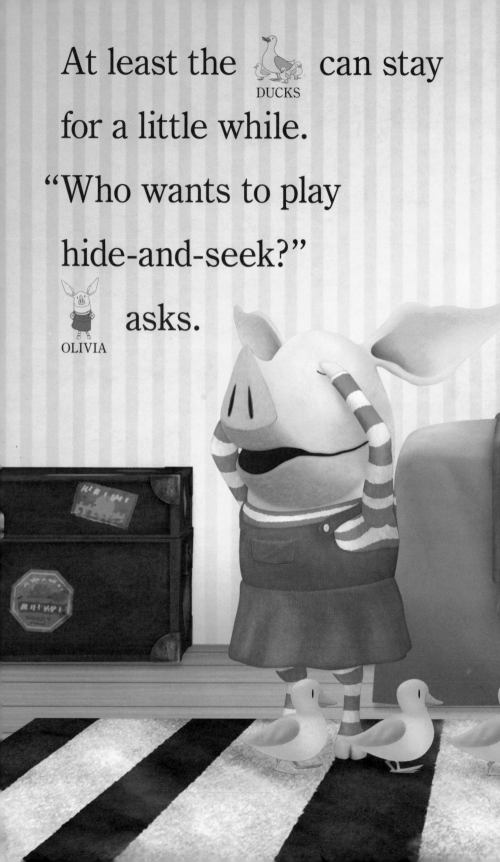 DUCKS can stay for a little while. "Who wants to play hide-and-seek?" OLIVIA asks.

"I do!" says 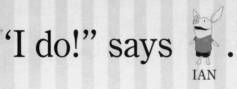.

IAN

"Don't look behind the !"

PIANO

 shuts her eyes.

OLIVIA

She counts to three.

looks in the kitchen.

OLIVIA

She does not see any 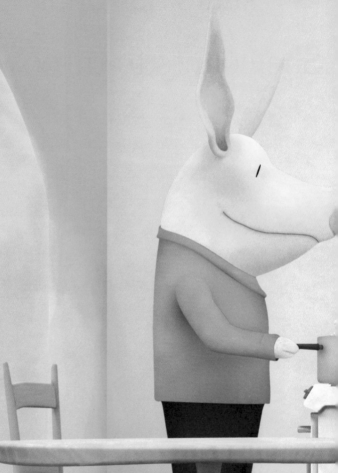 .

DUCKS